MW00914987

To

Giulia

From

Granny Barbara
and
Uncle Bill

THE
SCRAWNY LITTLE TREE

A CHRISTMAS STORY

by Ed Mehler
illustrated by Susie Pollard

PSS!
PRICE STERN SLOAN
An Imprint of Penguin Group (USA) Inc.

Dedicated to the children . . .

One Christmas Eve some years ago
a legend came to be,
a miracle, some people say,
and most others will agree.

In a little town not far from here,
it happened in this way
that love was given by a boy
and returned to him that day.

Though cheers of "Merry Christmas!" rang
from people everywhere,
for some 'twas not a happy day,
but no one seemed to care.

Most children laughed and sang their songs,
their trees stood proud and tall.
Boxes filled their living rooms
with gifts to them from all.

No thought was given to the ones
who lived a life so bare,
with all money used to pay for food
and nothing left to spare.

People went to buy their trees,
which stood in rows of green,
the finest ones in many years
that anyone had seen.

There, a little tree so frail and small
was placed behind the rest.
Fading needles sparsely seen
on tiny limbs were pressed.

Unnoticed by the milling throng,
a tear fell from a limb.
The little tree was saddened so
that no one wanted him.

Until one day a little boy
with torn and shabby dress
stood before the little tree
and smiled with happiness.

The little boy with arms so small
saved pennies, though very poor,
to buy himself a Christmas tree,
which he'd never had before.

Though he admired the other trees
with needles thick and green,
he felt compassion for this one,
to others there unseen.

The skinny limbs were like his own,
and height about the same.
The love he felt grew deep within
and kindled like a flame.

To him that scrawny little tree,
now standing all alone,
was just the tree he'd dreamed about,
with a beauty all its own.

He gave his pennies to the man,
though a very small amount.
The man grabbed them, laughed out loud,
and didn't even count.

The little boy picked up the tree
and, holding it so tight,
took it to his tiny shack
to stand in plainest sight.

He placed it there before the door
so everyone could see
and, sitting till the darkness came,
admired his little tree.

He slipped into his little bed,
a smile upon his face.
He said his prayers to the Lord
and thanked Him for His grace.

How proud he was, this lonely lad—
a Christmas tree at last!
Nothing else would matter now,
and sleep came very fast.

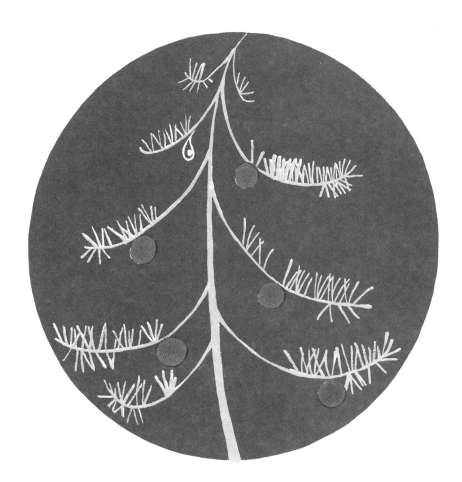

The little tree still shed a tear,
but it was a tear of joy.
He felt contentment deep inside—
how he loved that little boy!

He felt so grateful for the love
that he had found that day,
he wanted to express his own,
that he somehow could repay.

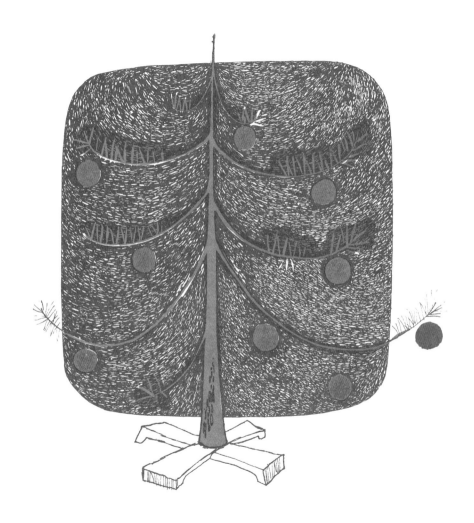

The feeling in his branches small
made his spirits soar.
A strange elation came o'er him
that he'd never felt before.

The love extended to his needles;
they now began to shine.
The proudness surged up through his trunk,
now held so straight and fine.

All through the night, the boy slept
and dreamed about the tree.
The thing he wanted most of all
now had come to be.

People said they'd never seen
the stars to shine so bright.
And the brightest one shone on that shack
throughout that wondrous night.

And when the boy awoke at dawn
to look upon his prize,
he rose and stood beneath the tree
but could not believe his eyes!

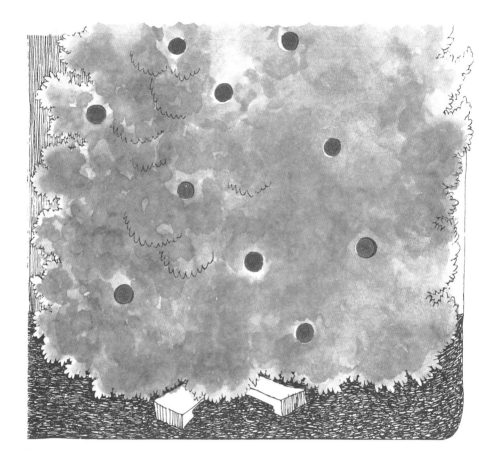

For in the spot where he had placed
the scrawny little tree
stood the most majestic one
in all of history!

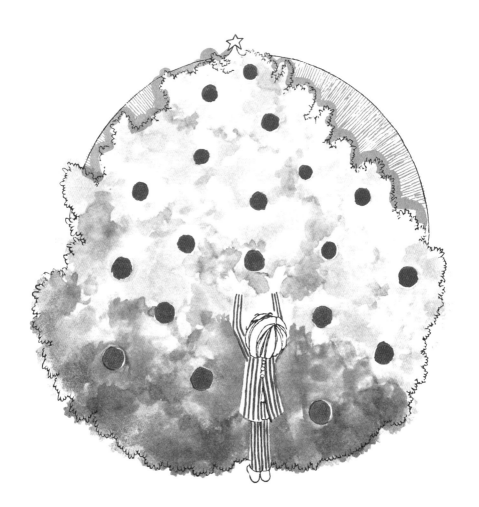

The greenest needles on shapely limbs
of perfect symmetry
grew from the trunk so straight and tall,
as high as he could see.

It seemed to hold a store of love,
which caused it to emit
a lovely glow of warmest light
that illuminated it.

The people passing by the shack
were stopped by what they saw.
They gathered there so silently,
and gazed in wondrous awe.

It wasn't long before the town
heard of this happening.
People came from near and far
to see this magic thing.

The beauty of the lonely tree
lent contrast to the shack
and to the tattered little boy
with rags upon his back.

This tiny boy beneath the tree
of such a giant size
made the people suddenly
begin to realize . . .

. . . that there are some who have no more
than love that they can give,
and ask for nothing in return
but peaceful lives to live.

The town, while captured by the sight
created by the tree,
felt sick at heart because the boy
lived in such misery.

The tree, they thought, must certainly
be kept for years to come,
for many others to behold
as they'd already done.

But they swore that boys and girls
like this would never spend
another Christmas Day in tears
alone, without a friend.

Many years have passed away,
but now the people care,
and Christmastime brings happiness
for children everywhere.

Boys and girls, both rich and poor,
now feel the kindness flow,
brought by a tree and a little boy
that day so long ago.

The little boy with tattered dress
is but a memory,
but something that he gave to us
will never cease to be.

And the tree they planted in the town
stands prouder than before,
a reminder of the power of love,
to stand forevermore.

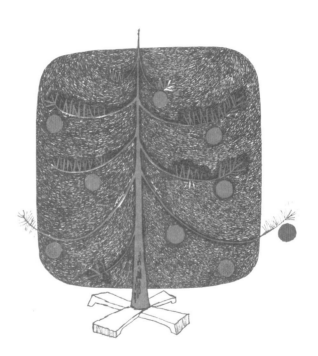